Worried Arthur

The Birthday Party

Ladybird books are widely available, but in case of difficulty may be ordered by post or telephone from:
Ladybird Books – Cash Sales Department Littlegate Road Paignton Devon TQ3 3BE Telephone 01803 554761

A catalogue record for this book is available from the British Library

Published by Ladybird Books Ltd Loughborough Leicestershire UK

Worried Arthur
The Birthday Party

by Joan Stimson

illustrated by Jan Lewis

Ladybird

Arthur was a penguin and a worrier. He knew that most things turned out well in the end but he still couldn't help *worrying*.

One morning Arthur woke up feeling excited and worried all at once. Dad had promised him a birthday party. And there were invitations to write.

All that day Arthur chewed the end of his pencil.
At last he finished his guest list.

"Now, what sort of party would you like Arthur?"
asked Dad.

Arthur wriggled happily. This was something he had *finished* worrying about.

"A bouncy iceberg party please, Dad," he said.

That night Arthur practised bouncing on his bed.

But the next day he flew in from school in a flap.

"Whatever is it?" asked Dad.

"It's Ben!" cried Arthur. "He's got such a big beak. And, when he biffed Flip's ball, he burst it. What if Ben bursts the bouncy iceberg at my party?"

"Good Heavens! That would never do," agreed Dad.
"Now, have you got any other ideas Arthur?"

Arthur smiled. He certainly had!

"A fancy dress party please, Dad," he said.

That evening Dad made
Arthur's costume.

It was perfect for Arthur.

In fact it was so perfect that Arthur insisted on wearing it to bed.

But the next day he tore in from school in a tantrum.

"Whatever is it, Arthur?" asked Dad.

"It's Wally," wailed Arthur. "*He's* having a fancy dress party, too. And Wally's birthday's before mine."

"That *is* unfortunate," agreed Dad. "But you can still wear your new costume to Wally's party. Now, have you got any *other* ideas Arthur?"

Arthur squirmed and wriggled. Then he disappeared. When he came back, he was wearing his trunks.

"A swimming party please, Dad," he said.

That evening Dad tried on *his* trunks. And Arthur found his snorkel.

But the next day Arthur was late home from school. At last he trudged indoors.

"Whatever is it *now*?" asked Dad.

"It's Katie," mumbled Arthur. "Katie can't swim yet. So it wouldn't be fair to have a swimming party."

"Quite right, too!" agreed Dad. "Now, have you got any *other* ideas Arthur?"

Arthur shuffled and shook his head.

"I've run out, Dad," he whispered.

"DON'T WORRY, Arthur!" cried Dad. "I'm sure we'll think of something."

Halfway through supper
Dad had a brainwave.

"I know," he beamed.
"You can have a
SURPRISE party!"

"Yippee!" cried Arthur.
"Will it be a surprise
for me, too?"

"Of course," said Dad.
"And this party will
suit EVERYONE."

Please come to Arthur's party Saturday 3 o'clock

Before bed Arthur wrote
out his invitations.
And the next morning
he took them to school.

The night before his party Arthur was so excited he didn't know what to do with himself.

"I can't wait to find out what the surprise is," he whispered. Then, all of a sudden, his face fell.

"Whatever is it?" asked Dad.

"Oh, Dad!" groaned Arthur. "You're not going to do your magic tricks are you… the ones that all go wrong?"

Dad coughed and spluttered.

"For your information, Arthur, my magic tricks are highly entertaining."

"But I do know better," he went on, "than to expect a group of growing penguins to sit still long enough to enjoy them!"

Arthur wriggled with relief and went off to bed.

When Arthur woke up, it was his birthday. And he was almost too busy to worry about his party.

There was a special birthday breakfast...

and presents...

and helping with the food…

…and finding his best tie.

All Arthur's guests arrived early. They wanted to know what the surprise was.

Just at that moment Dad staggered downstairs.
He was carrying a HUGE cardboard box.

Inside were some old curtains, several pieces of wood, some coloured ribbon, a ball of string and a pot of glue.

Arthur's guests looked confused.

Arthur was in a panic. "Oh no," he groaned. "It's the magic tricks after all!"

But then Arthur's dad made an announcement:

"Welcome," he began in an impressive voice, "to Arthur's... outstandingly rated... fresh-air related... uncomplicated... do-it-yourself...

KITE PARTY!"

Arthur and his friends made up their kites in record time. With whoops and shrieks they raced along the seashore.

Then they ran back inside and *demolished* the birthday food.

By the time Arthur waved goodbye to his guests, he was beginning to yawn. Dad was yawning, too.

"And how did you enjoy your party?" he asked Arthur.

"Oh Dad!" cried Arthur. "It was MAGIC!"

But there's just *one* thing worrying me," he whispered.

"What is it, Arthur?" asked Dad wearily.

"Well, Dad, will you be able to think of another surprise in time for next year?"

Dad smiled. "Just relax, Arthur," he said. "And let *me* do the worrying."